To Perry

Happy Chanukah
Merry Christmas
2004
Love
Crick, Sarah, Rachel + Bryan

HORNED TOAD
CANYON

For my grandson, Trey,

top hand of Crosswinds-Bar

bright sky press
Box 416
Albany, Texas 76430

10   9   8   7   6   5   4   3   2   1

Library of Congress Cataloging-in-Publication Data

Roach, Joyce Gibson
    Horned Toad Canyon / by Joyce Gibson Roach ; illustrations by Charles Shaw.
      p. cm.
      Summary: After a cattle stampede, the horned toads, rattlesnakes, hawks, and other residents of Horned Toad Canyon begin to put their homes back in order, not knowing that more trouble is headed their way.
      ISBN 1-931721-01-7 (alk. paper)
      [1. Horned toads—Fiction. 2. Desert animals—Fiction. 3. Cattle—Fiction. 4. Cowboys—Fiction. 5. Southwest, New—Fiction.] I. Shaw, Charles, 1941– ill. II. Title.

PZ7.R5275Ho 2003
[Fic]—dc21

                                                                                    2003049557

Map and drawings by illustrator after Sherbrooke, <u>Horned Lizards: Unique Reptiles of Western North America,</u> by Wade C. Sherbrooke, published by Southwest Parks and Monument Association, Globe, Arizona, 1981.

Book and cover design by Isabel Lasater Hernandez

Printed in China through Asia Pacific Offset

By Joyce Gibson Roach

HORNED TOAD CANYON

Illustrated by Charles Shaw

Just before the sun looked over the edge of earth, night hunters already knew that day was coming. Coyotes and bobcats, raccoons and foxes, mice and skunks returned to their homes in dens, holes and burrows.

Tecolote, the owl, whose short name was Teco, circled for the last time over Horned Toad Canyon to see what might still be about. Harris Hawk would take up the lookout after dawn. The rocky place, named for the many horned lizards that lived here, sheltered them all—animals, birds, reptiles and insects.

The tiny, spiny ones were not up and out yet. Like other reptiles, horned lizards have no way to make their own body heat, and so they stayed underground until the sun warmed the earth and them.

As always, the sun rose, sending summer heat above and below ground. Then, just as the horned lizards were beginning to warm up, stretch and wriggle, the ground began to tremble. A rumble like thunder shook the sand where they were buried.

"Rain, maybe," said their leader Tuck as he stuck his head out of the sand. "We could use a little rain."

But rain didn't come. Tuck saw only sunshine. There was not a cloud in the sky, but the thunder grew louder and nearer.

Other horned lizards appeared, some from under rocks and sagebrush, others from under tree roots, prickly pear cactus and bunchgrass.

"What's that?" asked Beam.

"What in blazes is goin' on?" shouted Shine.

"Whoever it is better watch out!" bellowed Digger. He arched his back, raised up on his front legs and hopped boldly a time or two.

"I'm not comin' out until somebody tells me what's goin' on."—this from Shorty who was scared of his own shadow and wouldn't move until somebody said it was okay.

"You won't come out even when we do tell you it's safe," snapped Nip. "You're such a …" but Nip didn't finish.

Along with the rolling thunder now a cloud of dust was moving toward the place where the horned toads lived. From the middle of the cloud came mooing and bawling, snorting and bellowing.

"Cattle!" yelled Tuck.

And there were other noises, whistling, yelling and the whir of ropes. Part of the clamor was from cattle and part from cowboys and horses, but the swirling, dusty racket was heading right toward the place where the horned lizards lived.

"Run!" shouted Digger.

The dirt moved violently. Scorpions, bugs and beetles crept, crawled and scurried for cover or dug in deeper. Grasshoppers swirled upward with the sand, crying "bz-z-z-clp, bz-z-z-clp" as they flew. Birds took to the sky.

Tuck and his friends were terrified by the terrible clatter of the quivering earth. Would they be trampled and crushed? Would their homes be destroyed? They buried themselves deep in the sand to wait out the danger.

The noisy rumbling and shaking went on and on. All the creatures and critters living in the dry, rocky, brushy place were tumbled, jostled and bumped.

After a while the rumble and roar moved farther away, and Horned Toad Canyon grew quiet and still.

One by one the lizards came back to the surface, sticking their heads out of the sand, but all moved cautiously in case they had to make a hasty retreat back underground.

Tuck called roll. "Beam, is Shine with you? Are you hurt?" The two were always together.

"I'm here," whispered Shine, but Beam did not say anything. "Oh, dear. Beam, where are you, where are you?" wailed Shine.

"I'm right here on the other side of the rock."

"Thank goodness," sighed Beam's best friend.

From other locations, Digger and Nip reported, "Yes, we're here."

Beam, Shine and Digger all spoke at the same time. "Who is it?" "What is it?" "Where is it, whatever it is?"

"Muffle, spiz, poofer, soo!" mumbled Shorty.

About that time, Buzz, the rattler, slithered from under a boulder. It took a big rock to hide Buzz because he was a very long rattlesnake.

"That's Shorty making that noise," said the snake. "He's buried so deep in a hole close to mine that you can't understand what he's sayin'. He refuses to come out. I tried to talk to him but … well, you know Shorty. Maybe you can do something with him, Nip."

"You bet I will," snapped Nip. Nip was the only one who could talk some sense into the stubborn lizard. "Shorty, you come out of there right now, do you hear? I mean right this minute!"

"Zuzzle, spoo, nana, no, I don't want to." Shorty's words became clearer the closer he got to the surface. "Oh, all right! Here I am, but I'm not staying long. The end of the world came, didn't it?"

"If it was the end of the world, then why are all of us still here?" asked Digger. "Well, what did happen, Tuck?"

"I don't know. I heard more than I saw. I was down in the sand with everybody else. Harris Hawk could tell us if …"

Right on cue, Harris plunged from the sky at high speed and made a precarious landing on a mesquite limb. The hawk wobbled awhile to get his balance.

"Whoops," said Harris. "I've got to be more careful." Harris was a large hawk whose wings spanned nearly four feet. "Are you folks okay? Anybody hurt?"

"We're okay, but tell us what happened. I thought we were going to get some rain. We could surely use it." Whatever else Tuck might have to say, he always mentioned rain.

"It was a cattle drive that went wrong," Harris explained. "The lead bull, Old Blue, got spooked by a dirt-devil or something and started runnin'. Then the other cattle followed until there was a regular stampede."

"Well, let's take a look around and check out the damage. Then we'll see what we can do about it," said Tuck cheerfully. No matter how bad the situation, Tuck always looked on the bright side.

He remembered once when a tornado tore down trees, swept away everything but the biggest rocks and blew piles and piles of sand into the air. When the spiral wind moved on, the toads discovered all kinds of stuff that hadn't been there before, and things that had been there were now gone.

Another time it didn't rain for months. The drought caused the river south of their grounds to dry up, leaving only a deep hole or two for all the animals to drink out of. Horned lizards usually watered on dew, but it got so hot and dry during the drought that there was little moisture on leaf or grass.

Grandparents told about a great flood when it rained for days and days. The water swept over the rocks and plants, destroying homes and dens and the ant beds on which horned lizards feed. It was then that they moved to Horned Toad Canyon.

Tuck knew that hailstorms and prairie fires caused great troubles through the years. Yet all managed to get by and go on with their lives. The stampede was only the most recent fright.

"I think we are safe now. Let's get busy. We have a lot to do." Like any good leader, Tuck made a plan and gave everybody an assignment. The others were good followers and would help each other. All, that is, except Shorty, who would not come out. He uncovered and reburied himself over and over.

Harris Hawk sat on his branch and studied the horned toads for a while longer. They were a great curiosity in a land filled with curious and strange creatures. By any standards, the horny toads, or horned frogs, or horned lizards—they were called by several names—were funny looking.

They didn't have beautiful wings like his. They had short stubby legs, round, flat bodies and a tail. Watching them run was a strange sight. Except for underneath their tummies, they were covered all over with spines. Their heads had a crown of sharp horns. And they had such odd habits.

After a day of hurrying and scurrying about the rocks and feeding on red ants caught by flicking out their tongues, the lizards would bury themselves in the sand or sit beneath the shade of yucca, grass or cactus. Their colors blended in with the colors of the arid landscape, making them very hard to see.

The horned frogs had natural enemies, but when threatened by animals, birds, snakes or anything else, they pushed themselves up on their front legs and looked fierce as if ready to charge. They could also fill their bodies full of air so they looked like fat toads. It made them hard to swallow, too.

Mostly the horned toads just bluffed, but they did have one trick that surprised their enemies. They could shoot blood out of their eyes and aim it forward or backward!

Harris Hawk ruffled his rusty-colored feathers and shuddered. He was very glad that Tuck or the others never pulled that awful trick on him.

The bird finally grew tired of watching and took to the air, waiting for the cool of evening when mice stirred and offered hope of supper.

Wind was always blowing in Horned Toad Canyon—Winter, Summer, Spring and Autumn—and never stopped. In fact, it was she, along with Harris Hawk, who brought them news and information from places far away and let them know what was going on.

In the late afternoon, just two days after the stampede, Wind appeared suddenly, spinning a dirt-devil into the middle of their camp. "Whee-ee-ee," Wind screeched as she scattered stinging sand all over them. "Take cover. A mama cow and her calf are coming this way. Guess they got separated from the herd."

Wind had no sooner spoken than Harris Hawk took off from his perch on the mesquite limb.

A calf, newborn from the looks of it, wobbled in, bawling weakly, "M-a-a, M-a-a, Ma-ma?"

"I'm right here behind you, dear," mooed the mother cow. She stepped carefully over the terrain, but stopped with her left foot squarely on top of some bunch grass where Shorty had his hole.

The horned lizards were not afraid of just one cow and calf. Strays sometimes wandered in.

"Excuse me, Ma'am" said Tuck, who was the first to make an appearance, "but you and the little one are standing on Shorty's house. Could you move just a tad to the right?"

"Why, of course," answered the mama cow as she nudged her baby with her nose. "My name is Emmaline, Em for short, and this is … well, I haven't thought of her name yet. She was born just as the stampede started. I was off a piece from the herd, and they took off without me. Cowboys will come looking for us soon."

Em is a very talkative cow, Tuck thought.

"Muffle, spoo, spiz?" came a sound from underground.

"What's that?" asked Em.

"Shorty, stop that nonsense. Come out of there. We've got company," shouted Nip.

Shorty's response was loud and clear, even from far underground. "Nope. No. Not!"

"Let him alone, Nip," begged Beam and Shine.

"Uh huh," Digger agreed.

"It's getting late," Tuck reminded them. "Let's get some sleep. Find yourself a spot, Em, and stay with us for the night. Tomorrow's another day."

"Um," murmured Digger, already half asleep.

As night fell, the full moon rose over Horned Toad Canyon, lighting the landscape in soft detail. Harris Hawk gave up Sky to Teco, who hunted at night and kept watch until dawn.

Lightning bugs blinked in the darkness.

Bats by the hundreds departed the crevices and caves of the canyon. They flew on black wings to feed on cacti, helping to pollinate the thorny plants with their nocturnal visits.

Wind's whispering cousin, Breeze, blew the evening noises up from the river.

"Whomp, whomp, whomp, whomp." The bullfrogs down by the river began the night song in their bass voices.

"Who? Whip-poor-will. Who? Whip-poor-will," asked and answered the night birds.

"I sure wish it would rain," murmured Tuck. "Maybe tomorrow."

The peaceful prairie scene was about to be disturbed the very next day, but the residents had no way of knowing that trouble of the worst kind was on the way.

Trouble had names, John and Juan. They had the same name, only in different languages. Juan was the Spanish word for John. But they didn't look anything alike. John was tall and freckle-faced, had blond hair and rode a little paint named Skyrocket. Juan was short, had brown skin and black hair and rode a big palomino called Tango. They were cowboys for the Crosswinds-Bar Ranch and were in trouble themselves—serious trouble.

"Juan, how do you suppose that stampede happened?"

"It was the fault of *el correcamino* more than the whirling sand," said Juan in Spanish. "I think maybe the bird thought it would be funny to make the cattle run. Roadrunners do silly things, like annoying animals by darting and dashing around."

"Well, Old Blue was plumb annoyed for sure," John said. "And now Boss is mad at us 'cause we let it happen. Cattle are scattered from the Brazos clear to the Pecos River, maybe. And Boss said not to come back 'til we found the strays—all of 'em."

Juan and John hadn't found a single stray all day, and neither was in a hurry to go back to the ranch until they found something.

Harris Hawk, circling lazily in the blue sky of afternoon, noticed movement far below. "Wonder what those two are up to? What are riders doing way out here?"

Harris knew about the strange creatures that walked on two legs but rode on the backs of four-legged animals most of the time. The sharp-eyed bird watched for a while longer, but the cowboys continued to ride closer and closer to the horned frogs' home. It was time to warn his friends.

The hawk, who never managed to land easily or quietly, nose-dived to earth with a screech. This time, Harris broke his favorite perch, fell with wings flapping and ended up in a cloud of dust. "Whoops! Sorry, but I've got to tell you …"

"Dadgum!" shouted Shorty who had just that very minute decided to make an appearance. Back he went, underground again. "Knew better, mutter, muffle, spif, soozle …"

"Oh, no," moaned Beam.

"Not again," sighed Shine.

"Now, look what you've done!" shouted Digger.

Em, who only minutes before had settled back down beneath a scrub oak tree after a breakfast of dry grass, jumped to her feet. She nosed her calf up and turned to face the squawking hawk. "I declare!" Em protested.

"Harris, we like your visits, but couldn't you be more careful?" asked Tuck, who rarely lost his good humor.

It took some time for things to settle down. There was a lot of running here and there, there and here. Em stayed on her feet, thinking it was better not to lie down again until the dust settled. Harris found another limb to sit on and watched the horned lizards. Matters were in such a mess, and he was the cause of it all. He completely forgot about why he had come in the first place. By the time he remembered, it was too late!

John and Juan moseyed right to the edge of the horned toads' camp. The cloud of dust caught their attention. Then they spotted Em and the calf getting up. *"¡La vaca! ¡Ándale!"* shouted Juan.

At the very same time, John said exactly the same words in English, "A cow! Hurry!" Then, "Shake out your rope and build a loop. I'll ride easy into the brush and see if I can move the cow your way. You'll never get a rope on her where she is."

Everything happened at once. Harris scrambled for the sky to save himself. The calf began to bawl as Em started to turn in a circle, not knowing from where the danger came. The horned lizards ran in every direction. There was no time to dig in.

Tuck, who always thought of something, didn't.

Nobody knew what to do, none except … except the one who lived under the boulder where John now rode Skyrocket.

Buzz wriggled from beneath the rock, coiled and shook his rattlers.

Skyrocket lived up to his name! The horse jumped skyward, bucking, leaping and plunging.

Emmaline, hearing Buzz's rattle, trotted away, knowing the calf would follow. Juan saw her move into the open. He dropped his *reata* perfectly over her horns.

"¡Perfecto!" yelled Juan, just as Skyrocket, with John holding on for dear life, flew by headed south for parts unknown.

"Vámonos, vámonos," shouted Juan as he herded Em and her calf toward the ranch.

It was late afternoon before most of the horned lizards who lived in Horned Toad Canyon finally returned to their homes. Breeze blew soft and warm from the south, rippling the grasses and waving the feathery mesquite leaves. Cicadas reported the temperature, while other insects droned and whispered.

After getting rid of humans, horses, a cow and calf, Buzz discovered he had worked up an appetite and slithered away to hunt.

The horned lizards spread out under cactus and sagebrush or near ant beds looking for supper.

Harris Hawk glided in, his coppery sunlit wings stretched out fully. He came quietly this time, perching on a different mesquite tree limb that wouldn't break easily.

Shorty, who had stayed underground during all the events, finally appeared. Not having eaten all day, he was starving and needed to find some ants.

"Nip? Beam? Shine?" He called but nobody answered.

"Digger? Tuck?" He listened but heard nothing. Somebody?"

Shorty sat by his left-lonesome self until evening. "Somebody?" he repeated over and over. "Anybody?"

Even Harris wouldn't say a word, fearful that he might cause another ruckus if he dared to move.

The moon began to rise as Tuck and the others returned at last.

"Oh, there you are," said Shorty with enthusiasm, but his pals were too tired to say a word.

"What happened? Tell me," begged Shorty. "Were you scared? What was all that noise?"

Nip, Tuck, Beam, Shine and Digger all began to dig into their holes. Nobody said a word.

"Somebody? Anybody? Harris?"

"Wait 'til morning," Tuck said as he burrowed into the sand. "Too tired. We'll talk tomorrow. There's always tomorrow."

As one by one, the horned lizards disappeared in the sand, Harris Hawk stretched his wings. He glided silently into the darkness of the canyon and gave the night to owl.

MORE ABOUT HORNED LIZARDS

Horned lizards, also called horned frogs, horny toads and horned toads, are reptiles. Their scientific name is *Phrynosoma* (frī-nō-sō-mă). In Greek, *phrynos* means toad and *soma* means body, or toad-bodied lizards.

Seven kinds of horned lizards are found, mostly in different parts of the Southwestern United States. Look at the drawings and map on the following page to see the differences between the types and where they are located.

Most horned lizards live in desert or semiarid places that are very hot. Some, however, live in the mountains, where it gets cool. Like other reptiles, they are cold-blooded and so depend on the place they live to regulate their body temperatures.

Wendy L. Hodges, a scientist who specializes in *Phrynosoma*, explains: "Reptiles and other 'cold-blooded' animals are really ectotherms. They do not produce heat inside their bodies and require an external heat source like the sun to help maintain body temperature. Birds and mammals are endotherms, meaning they have the ability to produce heat inside their bodies. Both endotherms and ectotherms try to maintain a fairly constant body temperature when they are active."

If a horned lizard becomes too hot underneath the sand, it may run from the surface to a shaded place. Sometimes they even climb into low-growing bushes in the hottest part of the day to maintain body temperature. If they get too cool, they may lie out in the sun for a while. Many of their activities have to do with keeping themselves at the right temperature.

Most horned lizards prefer large harvester ants to eat. The ants live in underground nests but spend the day going back and forth in columns to find and bring back food, mostly seeds. Horned lizards wait beside the trail or entrance to the nest, flick out their tongues, catch an ant and swallow without chewing it. One lizard may eat as many as 200 ants every day.

Horned lizards get most of their water from their food. They also lap up drops of dew or rainwater from plants or shallow places on rocks. If a horned lizard is out in the rain, it uses its body to collect water by arching its back and holding its head down. Drops of water are pulled into tiny channels in their scales, and gravity draws the water toward their mouths.

Fecal droppings, called scat, are composed of dead ant parts and are black or dark brown in color. At the end of the scat is a white urine dot. Urine is passed in this semi-solid form rather than liquid. This process helps the lizards retain more water in their bodies.

Generally, young horned lizards are active and feeding until early November when they begin to hibernate. Adults hibernate earlier because they already have enough body fat to sustain them through the winter. In April, most begin to come out of hibernation.

There are male and female horned lizards. They have courting rituals in which they do such things as bob their heads over and over again. Mating occurs in the springtime, and later, the female lays eggs in a kind of nest. She finds a good place with the right amount of sunshine, moisture, drainage and ventilation and then digs a slanted tunnel into the ground six to eight inches deep. After laying her eggs, the female covers the nest, stays for a little while and then goes away. She never knows whether her young have hatched or what happens to them.

Baby horned lizards have to work at hatching out of their eggs. They have a pointed tooth called the egg tooth with which they can make a hole in the egg. When they dig out to the surface they are on their own,

AMERICAN HORNED LI

COAST HORNED
LIZARD

SHORT HORNED
LIZARD

FLAT-TAIL
HORNED LIZARD

TEXAS HORNED LIZARD
THE TEXAS STATE REPTILE

RDS

REGAL
HORNED LIZARD

ROUND TAIL
HORNED LIZARD

DESERT
HORNED LIZARD

but somehow they know how to get food and water, keep warm or cool and avoid enemies.

Horned lizards have some natural enemies such as hawks, roadrunners, snakes, coyotes, ground squirrels, mice, cats and dogs. They avoid predators in several ways. Their colors help them blend in with the landscape, making them hard to see. They simply run and stop, which confuses their enemies; or they run away and bury themselves quickly. They bluff and may pretend to charge the enemy; or they inflate their bodies with air, making them too large to swallow. They sometimes raise up on all fours, lower their heads and hop toward the enemy like a charging bull. If a predator should happen to swallow a horned lizard, he risks getting the horns stuck in his throat.

Some horned toads can squirt blood from their eyes. They do this by first closing their eyelids, which begin to swell and fill with blood as pressure builds in their heads. Then they are able to shoot out a fine stream of blood for up to four feet. They can do this two or three times or more. The enemies of the horned lizard are startled and may lose interest. Or, if the blood gets into the eyes or mouth of predators, it feels or tastes bad, and they drop the lizard.

Horned lizards look fierce and resemble tiny dinosaurs, but they are very gentle creatures. If you pick one up, it will usually be very still in your hand. They cannot hurt people.

There are fewer horned lizards than there used to be. Many are disappearing from parts of the Southwest and some are on the wildlife Protected List. This means that it is not legal to keep, carry them around or sell them. Part of the reason is that the horned lizard's habitat is being destroyed because we are tearing up land for roads and buildings. Also, some pesticides are harmful to them.

It is best to leave horned lizards where they are in their natural habitat, observe and study them as biologists do and think about these unusual, harmless creatures of the Southwest.

The earliest stories about *Phrynosoma* appeared in prehistoric art forms of the earliest cultures of the Southwest hundreds of years ago. The Anasazi, Mogollon and Hohokam peoples of the desert regions of Texas, New Mexico and Arizona painted images of horned lizards on cave walls and cliff dwellings. They marked pottery and carved petroglyphs into the surfaces of rocks with the design. They sculpted spiny creatures of clay and carved their likeness out of minerals and stone, called fetishes, and used them to help cure illnesses.

The descendants of these prehistoric peoples made use of horned lizards in their stories and legends. The Pima thought horned lizards had the ability to change health and believed they could bring happiness. They could be dangerous if people offended or hurt them. There were those who knew how to sing the horned lizard songs and tell the stories about them.

A Zuni tale tells of sacred horned lizards that are life-sized and can laugh. Even today, the Zuni are well known for carving the horned lizard from mineral and stone and for using the design in silver jewelry, such as pins.

The Navajo tell a story about a wicked coyote who was jealous of a horned toad's good farm, clean hogan and garden. Coyote went to the horned lizard's house and took his things. Then he swallowed the spiny creature, but he later died because the horns stuck in his throat.

The Navajo also made use of horned lizards in sacred sand paintings that were used as part of curing or blessing ceremonies.

The Comanche and other Plains tribes consulted horned lizards to ask where buffalo were located. Whichever way they ran told the direction to take to find the buffalo.

The Spanish noticed horned lizards while on a scientific expedition to the New World and reported on them as early as 1651. Meriwether Lewis observed them on the famous Lewis and Clark expedition in 1804. Lewis sent a specimen back to Thomas Jefferson who had it placed in the first natural history museum. The French explorers called horned lizards "prairie buffalo" because of the horns and humping of the back when they were upset.

English-speaking children have more than one name for *Phrynosoma*, such as horny toad, horned toad and horned frog. In Spanish they are known as *torito de la Virgen*, little bull who protects the Virgin, because they charge when facing enemies. In spite of their tiny size, they are regarded as sacred because they seem to cry tears of blood.

Largartito, little alligator, and *sapo con quernitos*, toad with horns, are other labels. The Mexican name is *cameleon*, perhaps because of its camouflage coloring.

Horned lizards are still a part of our culture. Some schools even have them as their mascot. TCU in Fort Worth, Texas, selected the horned frog as its mascot and totem way back in 1897. Many of them roamed Thorp Spring, the original site of the university. They knew the little critter was tough, tenacious, and willing to tackle enemies bigger than they, even if bluffing and looking mean were their only defenses.

Whether scientists study them, people tell stories about them or use them in artistic forms, horned lizards are important to us. Wade Sherbrooke, another scientist who studies horned lizards, says that, "the mother of all life twinkles in the eyes of horned lizards too. For the story of horned lizards is not an isolated one. Are they not, like us, but another color in the rainbow of life shining out of the past through the prism of time, and onward into the unknown future?"

GLOSSARY

arid: hot, very dry; arid places do not get much rain.
Brazos and Pecos Rivers: important rivers located in West Texas, whose headwaters are in New Mexico.
bunchgrass: any of a number of grasses that grow in clumps or bunches suitable for cattle and other grazing animals.
canyon: a narrow depression in the earth with very steep sides where a river runs through it or where large amounts of water have passed through at some time; may be dry; other names are gulch and draw.
cicada: also called *locust;* large insect with four wings; male produces a long, whirring, chirping sound during hot weather that is believed to get louder as the temperature gets hotter.
dirt-devil: sometimes called dust-devil or whirlwind; a spiraling wind

composed of dirt and other particles that moves across the landscape like a miniature tornado but causes no damage.

Harris Hawk: a large hawk, or raptor, named after Edward Harris; has reddish, coppery wings with chestnut color underneath and has a wingspan of four feet; nests in low trees or yucca and lives in the brush lands and mesquite thickets of the Southwestern United States and Mexico.

harvester ants: large ants, reddish brown or black in color; not fire ants.

hogan: a Navajo house; round, rather than square, and made of logs.

nocturnal: another word for nighttime.

petroglyph: a picture or figure carved on a rock

pollinate: to move pollen from one part of a flower to another part of the same flower; or from one flower to a different one.

prickly pear: a type of cactus with sharp spines and fine "stickers" all over the surface that keep cattle from eating it and keep other animals away; used by some birds, especially wrens, to nest in; plural of cactus is cacti.

COWBOY LINGO

a tad: a little bit

a piece: some distance away

build a loop: to make a circle of rope

dadgum: a funny word to say when you're surprised or a little out of sorts

mosey: to move slowly and easily; not in a hurry

plumb: completely; very

shake out your rope: to take the coiled rope off the saddle horn and shake it loose

stampede: when cattle become frightened or startled by something and start running

Ma'am: old fashioned, abbreviated word for Madam, or Mrs.

SPANISH WORDS

ándale: hurry

el correcamino: the roadrunner, or chaparral cock

la vaca: a cow, or the cow

perfecto: just right, perfect

reata: lasso or rope used to catch cattle or horses

vámonos: let's go

AZTEC WORDS *incorporated into the Spanish language*

coyote: from the Aztec word, *coyotl*

tecolote: from the Aztec word *tecolotl*

WHERE TO FIND OUT MORE

Horned Lizards by Jane Manaster, Texas Tech University Press, Lubbock; contains history, natural science and folklore with multi-cultural perspectives; color photographs and illustrations.

Horned Lizards: Unique Reptiles of Western North America by Wade Sherbrooke published by Southwest Parks and Monuments Association, Globe, Arizona; scientific information, maps and color photographs.

Introduction to Horned Lizards of North America by Wade Sherbrooke, University of California Press.

The Roadrunner by Wyman Meinzer, Texas Tech University Press, Lubbock; information and extraordinary photographs of this unique bird of the Southwest that include horned lizards.

Horned Lizard Conservation Society, PO Box 122, Austin, Texas 78767.

Horned Lizard Conservation Society website, http://www.hornedlizards.org

Email, phrynosoma@hornedlizards.org